THIS BOOK
BELONGS TO:

. . . .

(WHOSE MISCHIEVOUS NATURE
MAY BENEFIT FROM THE
TALES WITHIN)

A Mischievous Little Rabbit

A Mischievous Little Rabbit

Tales of
Danger and
Daring

WARNE

FREDERICK WARNE

Published by the Penguin Group
Penguin Books Ltd, 80 Strand, London WC2R oRL, England
Penguin Group (USA) Inc., 375 Hudson Street, New York, New York 10014, USA
Penguin Books Australia Ltd, 250 Camberwell Road, Camberwell, Victoria 3124, Australia
Penguin Books Canada Ltd, 90 Eglinton Avenue East, Suite 700, Toronto, Ontario, Canada M4P 2Y3
Penguin Books India (P) Ltd, 11 Community Centre, Panchsheel Park, New Delhi 110 017, India
Penguin Books (NZ) Ltd, 67 Apollo Drive, Rosedale, North Shore 0632, New Zealand
Penguin Books (South Africa) (Pty) Ltd, 24 Sturdee Avenue, Rosebank, Johannesburg 2196, South Africa

Penguin Books Ltd, Registered Offices: 80 Strand, London WC2R oRL, England

Web site at: www.peterrabbit.com

First published by Frederick Warne 2011
001-1 3 5 7 9 10 8 6 4 2

ISBN 978-0-72326-785-0

Colour reproduction by MDP (Media, Development and Printing Ltd.)
Printed and bound in China

CONTENTS

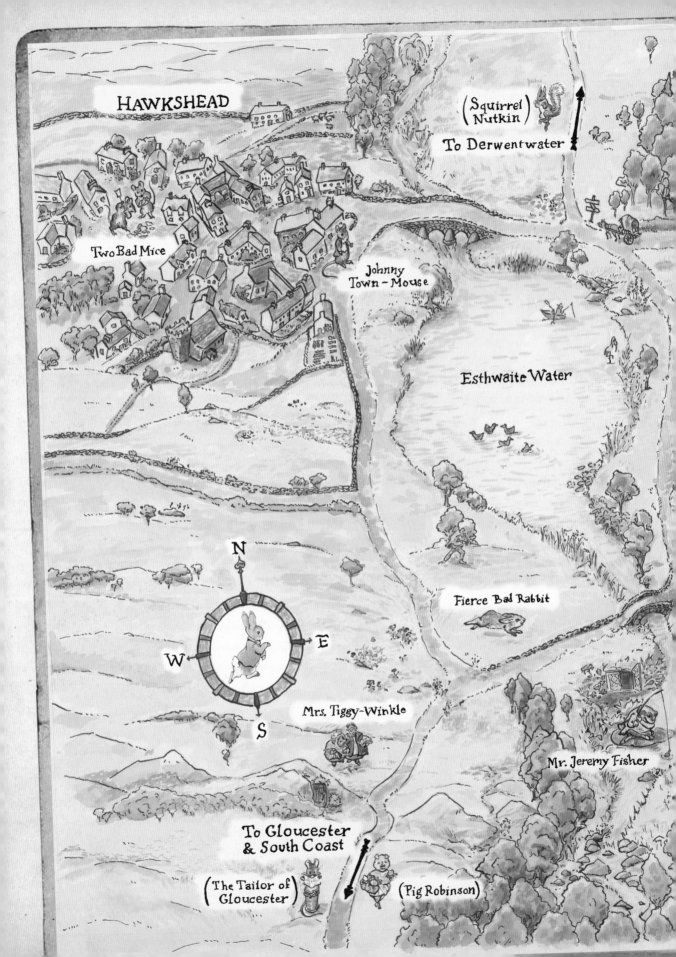

HAWKSHEAD

Two Bad Mice

(Squirrel Nutkin)

To Derwentwater

Johnny Town-Mouse

Esthwaite Water

N

W   E

S

Fierce Bad Rabbit

Mrs. Tiggy-Winkle

Mr. Jeremy Fisher

To Gloucester & South Coast

(The Tailor of Gloucester)

(Pig Robinson)

MAP OF
BEATRIX POTTER'S
WORLD

Mr. Tod's
Winter House

L BANKS

Duchess

Ginger &
Pickles'
Shop

The Tower
Bank Arms

Ribby

VREY

Timmy
Willie

To Lake Windermere

Hill Top
Farm

Samuel Whiskers

Tom Kitten,
Miss Moppet
& Family

Barn

Jemima
Puddle-duck

Mr. Tod's
Summer House

Pigling Bland

Mr. McGregor's
Garden

Mrs. Tittlemouse

Peter Rabbit

nmy
toes

Benjamin
Bunny

The
Flopsy Bunnies

Who's Who in Our Tales

Peter Rabbit

Speed – A fast runner, better on four legs than two.

Escaping – A masterful escaper.

Making mischief – Peter can be very mischievous, more so when he is with his cousin, Benjamin Bunny.

Likes: Finding his way into Mr. McGregor's vegetable garden.

Dislikes: Finding his way out again.

Tailor of Gloucester

Speed – quite elderly and not fast on his feet.

Escaping – The kindly tailor has never needed to escape, although the mice living in his house have.

Making mischief – only Simpkin, the tailor's cat, makes mischief, but he is mischievous enough for everyone.

Likes: Making clothes for the fine people of Gloucester.

Dislikes: Being unable to work.

Jeremy Fisher

Speed – Expert leaper and swimmer.

Escaping – He has had many lucky escapes. He is a fortunate frog.

Making mischief – He likes a quiet life.

Likes: Sitting on a lily pad, catching minnows. His macintosh.

Dislikes: Very large trout.

Jemima Puddle-Duck

Speed – Not bad at flying once she gets going. Progress is slow if waddling.

Escaping – Only with help

Making mischief – Jemima is generally a very well behaved duck

Likes: Pottering about the farmyard.

Dislikes: Flying

Samuel Whiskers

Speed – Not fast, due to his liking for bacon.

Escaping – Quite quick if he is stealing something, like bacon.

Making mischief – Very mischievous

Likes: Teasing poor Tom Kitten

Dislikes: Cats

GINGER AND PICKLES

SPEED – Quick, when chasing 4-legged creatures smaller than them.

ESCAPING – Quite good, if they rely on biting and barking.

MAKING MISCHIEF – Ginger and Pickles run a respected retail establishment. They are not mischief makers.

LIKES: Providing provisions to the villagers.

DISLIKES: German doll policemen

TIMMY TIPTOES

SPEED – Fast, and a good climber

ESCAPING – Hopeless

MAKING MISCHIEF – He doesn't mean to be mischievous.

LIKES: Eating nuts

DISLIKES: Climbing out of small holes.

MR. TOD

SPEED – Deceptively fast, particularly if he's feeling peckish.

ESCAPING – Very good

MAKING MISCHIEF – Never mind mischievous – Mr Tod could EAT you.

LIKES: Slinking quietly through the woods, looking for trouble.

DISLIKES: Almost everyone.

PIGLING BLAND

SPEED – Not very fast. Perhaps a little too tubby.

ESCAPING – Quite good, but through luck rather than judgement.

MAKING MISCHIEF – Pigling Bland is a conscientious piglet.

LIKES: Eating, and making friends.

DISLIKES: Getting lost.

JOHNNY TOWN-MOUSE

SPEED – Being born in a city makes him fast on his feet.

ESCAPING – Very quick

MAKING MISCHIEF – As mischievous as the cat will allow.

LIKES: Hosting dinner parties

DISLIKES: Getting his shoes muddy.

About the Mischievous Miss Potter

Beatrix Potter was never one to follow convention and we have a few tales of her own mischievousness to relate to you...

When she was just a little girl, Beatrix smuggled a rabbit into the house in a paper bag and it remained in the nursery, undetected, for a week! Another time, she found it such hard work to cut the real Peter Rabbit's nails with small manicure scissors that she chose to use a pair of large garden scissors instead. (One can only imagine how poor Peter felt when confronted with them!)

The little hedgehog, Mrs. Tiggy-winkle, did not escape Beatrix's slightly impish behaviour either. When being used as a model, Beatrix would prop her up on one end for hours – not letting her go, even when she began to yawn and then eventually, bite!

Beatrix's naughty inclinations did not diminish with age. When visiting an old friend at Windemere, she took a basket and trowel with her, and mischievously admitted to taking something from every single garden in the village to plant in her own.

Knowing all this about Miss Potter, we can imagine the twinkle in her eye as she sat down to write these wonderful tales of daring and danger. Now let's turn the page and we'll begin...

THE TALE OF
PETER RABBIT

ONCE UPON A TIME there were four little Rabbits, and their names were —
>   Flopsy,
>   Mopsy,
>   Cotton-tail,
>   and Peter.
>   They lived with their Mother in a sand-bank, underneath the root of a very big fir-tree.

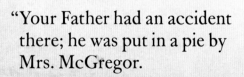

"Now, my dears," said old Mrs. Rabbit one morning, "you may go into the fields or down the lane, but don't go into Mr. McGregor's garden.

"Your Father had an accident there; he was put in a pie by Mrs. McGregor.

"Now run along, and don't get into mischief. I am going out."

Then old Mrs. Rabbit took a basket and her umbrella, and went through the wood to the baker's. She bought a loaf of brown bread and five currant buns.

Flopsy, Mopsy and Cotton-tail, who were good little bunnies, went down the lane to gather blackberries;

An old mouse was running in and out over the stone door-step, carrying peas and beans to her family in the wood. Peter asked her the way to the gate, but she had such a large pea in her mouth that she could not answer. She only shook her head at him. Peter began to cry.

Then he tried to find his way straight across the garden, but he became more and more puzzled. Presently, he came to a pond where Mr. McGregor filled his water-cans. A white cat was staring at some gold-fish; she sat very, very still, but now and then the tip of her tail twitched as if it were alive. Peter thought it best to go away without speaking to her; he had heard about cats from his cousin, little Benjamin Bunny.

He went back towards the tool-shed, but suddenly, quite close to him, he heard the noise of a hoe — scr-r-ritch, scratch, scratch, scritch. Peter scuttered underneath the bushes.

But presently, as nothing happened, he came out, and climbed upon a wheelbarrow, and peeped over. The first thing he saw was Mr. McGregor hoeing onions. His back was turned towards Peter, and beyond him was the gate!

Peter got down very quietly off the wheelbarrow, and started running as fast as he could go, along a straight walk behind some black-currant bushes.

Mr. McGregor caught sight of him at the corner, but Peter did not care. He slipped underneath the gate, and was safe at last in the wood outside the garden.

Mr. McGregor hung up the little jacket and the shoes for a scarecrow to frighten the blackbirds.

Peter never stopped running or looked behind him till he got home to the big fir-tree.

He was so tired that he flopped down upon the nice soft sand on the floor of the rabbit-hole, and shut his eyes. His mother was busy cooking; she wondered what he had done with his clothes. It was the second little jacket and pair of shoes that Peter had lost in a fortnight!

I am sorry to say that Peter was not very well during the evening.

His mother put him to bed, and made some camomile tea; and she gave a dose of it to Peter!

"One table-spoonful to be taken at bed-time."

But Flopsy, Mopsy, and Cotton-tail had bread and milk and blackberries for supper.

THE END

From this frightening day onwards, Peter tried hard to be a better behaved rabbit . . . →

Mrs. Rabbit's Weekly Reward Chart

	Flopsy	Mopsy	Cotton-tail	Peter
Helping around the burrow	✓	✓	✓	✗ Started. didn't finish.
Making your own bed	✓	✓	✓	✗ Started. didn't finish.
Helping at mealtimes	✓	✓	✓	✗
Doing as you are told	✓	✓	✓	✗
Not eating between meals	✓	✓	✓	✗

A currant bun at the end of the week for all good little bunnies.
Bed with ~~no~~ supper for naughty little rabbits.

THE TALE OF
JEMIMA
PUDDLE-DUCK

Jemima Puddle-duck was not much in the habit of flying. She ran downhill a few yards flapping her shawl, and then she jumped off into the air.

She flew beautifully when she had got a good start.

She skimmed along over the tree-tops until she saw an open place in the middle of the wood, where the trees and brushwood had been cleared.

Jemima alighted rather heavily, and began to waddle about in search of a convenient dry nesting-place.

She rather fancied a tree-stump amongst some tall fox-gloves.

But — seated upon the stump, she was startled to find an elegantly dressed gentleman reading a newspaper.

He had black prick ears and sandy-coloured whiskers.

"Quack?" said Jemima Puddle-duck, with her head and her bonnet on one side — "Quack?"

The gentleman raised his eyes above his newspaper and looked curiously at Jemima —

"Madam, have you lost your way?" said he. He had a long bushy tail which he was sitting upon, as the stump was somewhat damp.

Jemima thought him mighty civil and handsome. She explained that she had not lost her way, but that she was trying to find a convenient dry nesting-place.

"Ah! is that so? indeed!" said the gentleman with sandy whiskers, looking curiously at Jemima. He folded up the newspaper, and put it in his coat-tail pocket.

Jemima complained of the superfluous hen.

"Indeed? how interesting!

He had a bite on his ear and both the puppies were limping.

Jemima Puddle-duck was escorted home in tears on account of those eggs.

She laid some more in June, and she was permitted to keep them herself; but only four of them hatched.

Jemima Puddle-duck said that it was because of her nerves; but she had always been a bad sitter.

THE END

And what do you think was inside that whiskered gentleman's pocket all that time . . . ?

A DISH OF ROASTED DUCK FOR THE DISCERNING GENTLEMAN

A full grown duck is best an ELDERLY animal is fit onLY for stewing, and a duckLing is not worth the bother.

Select a duck with thick yellowish feet and a plump belly.

A plain roast duck is one of the most excellent of dishes. When roasted to perfection it should be just pink inside, whilst the flesh on the legs should fall away pleasingly from the bone. *DO NOT NEGLECT THE FEET. THEY ARE DELICIOUSLY CRUNCHY.*

INGREDIENTS

1 duck
2 onions
4 carrots
A small piece of turnip
A small piece of celery
Butter
Fresh herbs

VEGetables and herbs in farm garden.

Dusk a good time to Raid dairy for butter

METHOD

First pluck your duck. All feathers must be removed – it is not pleasant to find stray feathers in your meal. With a sharp cook's knife, chop off its head at the base of the neck.

KEEP feathers in wood shed, for EntiCEMEnt purposes.

Using nimble paws, separate the skin from the flesh at the back of the neck to form a small pocket. Stuff your duck. *(SAGE AND ONION STUFFING IS PREFERABLE.)*

Lay your duck in a roasting tin and add your vegetables, finely diced, and a bunch of fresh herbs.

Place in a hot oven, and cook for about 2 hours. Keep bird well basted with melted butter to ensure the meat is tasty and succulent. When serving your roasted duck, be sure to retain the fat. This is delicious on toast. *(SOME DUCKS ARE VERY FAT.)*

Carve into elegant long pieces.

When in season, green peas should invariably accompany this dish.

THE TALE OF
MR. TOD

I HAVE MADE MANY BOOKS about well-behaved people. Now, for a change, I am going to make a story about two disagreeable people, called Tommy Brock and Mr. Tod.

Nobody could call Mr. Tod "nice". The rabbits could not bear him; they could smell him half a mile off. He was of a wandering habit and he had foxy whiskers; they never knew where he would be next.

One day he was living in a stick-house in the coppice, causing terror to the family of old Mr. Benjamin Bouncer. Next day he moved into a pollard willow near the lake, frightening the wild ducks and the water rats.

In winter and early spring he might generally be found in an earth amongst the rocks at the top of Bull Banks, under Oatmeal Crag.

He had half a dozen houses, but he was seldom at home.

The houses were not always empty when Mr. Tod moved *out*; because sometimes Tommy Brock moved *in*; (without asking leave).

Tommy Brock was a short bristly fat waddling person with a grin; he grinned all over his face. He was not nice in his habits. He ate wasp nests and frogs and worms; and he waddled about by moonlight, digging things up.

His clothes were very dirty; and as he slept in the day-time, he always went to bed in his boots. And the bed which he went to bed in, was generally Mr. Tod's.

Now Tommy Brock did occasionally eat rabbit-pie; but it was only very little young ones occasionally, when other food was really scarce. He was friendly with old Mr. Bouncer; they agreed in disliking the wicked otters and Mr. Tod; they often talked over that painful subject.

Old Mr. Bouncer was stricken in years. He sat in the spring

sunshine outside the burrow, in a muffler; smoking a pipe of rabbit-tobacco.

He lived with his son Benjamin Bunny and his daughter-in-law Flopsy, who had a young family. Old Mr. Bouncer was in charge of the family that afternoon, because Benjamin and Flopsy had gone out.

The little rabbit babies were just old enough to open their blue eyes and kick. They lay in a fluffy bed of rabbit wool and hay, in a shallow burrow, separate from the main rabbit-hole. To tell the truth — old Mr. Bouncer had forgotten them.

He sat in the sun, and conversed cordially with Tommy Brock, who was passing through the wood

with a sack and a little spud which he used for digging, and some mole traps. He complained bitterly about the scarcity of pheasants' eggs, and accused Mr. Tod of poaching them. And the otters had

cleared off all the frogs while he was asleep in winter — "I have not had a good square meal for a fortnight, I am living on pig-nuts. I shall have to turn vegetarian and eat my own tail!" said Tommy Brock.

It was not much of a joke, but it tickled old Mr. Bouncer; because Tommy Brock was so fat and stumpy and grinning.

So old Mr. Bouncer laughed; and pressed Tommy Brock to come inside, to taste a slice of seed-cake and "a glass of my daughter Flopsy's cowslip wine". Tommy Brock squeezed himself into the rabbit-hole with alacrity.

Then old Mr. Bouncer smoked another pipe, and gave Tommy Brock a cabbage leaf cigar which was so very strong that it made Tommy Brock grin more than ever; and the smoke filled the burrow. Old Mr. Bouncer coughed and laughed; and Tommy Brock puffed and grinned.

And Mr. Bouncer laughed and coughed, and shut his eyes because of the cabbage smoke . . .

When Flopsy and Benjamin came back — old Mr. Bouncer woke up. Tommy Brock and all the young rabbit babies had disappeared!

Mr. Bouncer would not confess that he had admitted anybody into the rabbit-hole. But the smell of badger was undeniable; and there were round heavy footmarks in the sand. He was in disgrace; Flopsy wrung her ears, and slapped him.

Benjamin Bunny set off at once after Tommy Brock.

where Tommy Brock had gone to. He
was further annoyed by the jay bird which
followed him persistently. It flew from
tree to tree and scolded, warning every
rabbit within hearing that either a cat or
a fox was coming up the plantation. Once
when it flew screaming over his head —
Mr. Tod snapped at it, and barked.

He approached his house very carefully, with a large rusty key.
He sniffed and his whiskers bristled. The house was locked up, but
Mr. Tod had his doubts whether it was empty. He turned the rusty
key in the lock; the rabbits below could hear it. Mr. Tod opened the
door cautiously and went in.

The sight that met Mr. Tod's eyes
in Mr. Tod's kitchen made Mr. Tod
furious. There was Mr. Tod's chair,
and Mr. Tod's pie-dish, and his knife
and fork and mustard and salt-cellar
and his tablecloth that he had left
folded up in the dresser — all set out
for supper (or breakfast) — without
doubt for that odious Tommy Brock.

There was a smell of fresh earth and dirty badger, which
fortunately overpowered all smell of rabbit.

But what absorbed Mr. Tod's
attention was a noise — a deep slow
regular snoring grunting noise,
coming from his own bed.

He peeped through the hinges of
the half-open bedroom door. Then
he turned and came out of the house

in a hurry. His whiskers bristled and his coat-collar stood on end with rage.

For the next twenty minutes Mr. Tod kept creeping cautiously into the house, and retreating hurriedly out again. By degrees he ventured further in — right into the bedroom. When he was outside the house, he scratched up the earth with fury. But when he was inside — he did not like the look of Tommy Brock's teeth.

He was lying on his back with his mouth open, grinning from ear to ear. He snored peacefully and regularly; but one eye was not perfectly shut.

Mr. Tod came in and out of the bedroom. Twice he brought in his walking-stick, and once he brought in the coal-scuttle. But he thought better of it, and took them away.

When he came back after removing the coal-scuttle, Tommy Brock was lying a little more sideways; but he seemed even sounder asleep. He was an incurably indolent person; he was not in the least afraid of Mr. Tod; he was simply too lazy and comfortable to move.

Mr. Tod gingerly mounted a chair by the head of the bedstead. His legs were dangerously near to Tommy Brock's teeth.

He reached up and put the end of rope, with the hook, over the head of the tester bed, where the curtains ought to hang.

(Mr. Tod's curtains were folded up, and put away, owing to the house being unoccupied. So was the counterpane. Tommy Brock was covered with a blanket only.) Mr. Tod standing on the unsteady chair looked down upon him attentively; he really was a first prize sound sleeper!

It seemed as though nothing would waken him — not even the flapping rope across the bed.

Mr. Tod descended safely from the chair, and endeavoured to get up again with the pail of water. He intended to hang it from the hook, dangling over the head of Tommy Brock, in order to make a sort of shower-bath, worked by a string, through the window.

But naturally being a thin-legged person (though vindictive and sandy whiskered) — he was quite unable to lift the heavy weight to the level of the hook and rope. He very nearly overbalanced himself.

The snores became more and more apoplectic. One of Tommy Brock's hind legs twitched under the blanket, but still he slept on peacefully.

Mr. Tod and the pail descended from the chair without accident. After considerable thought, he emptied the water into a wash-basin and jug. The empty pail was not too heavy for him; he slung it up wobbling over the head of Tommy Brock.

Surely there never was such a sleeper! Mr. Tod got up and down, down and up on the chair.

As he could not lift the whole pailful of water at once, he fetched a milk jug, and ladled quarts of water into the pail by degrees. The pail got fuller and fuller, and swung like a pendulum. Occasionally a drop splashed over; but still Tommy Brock snored regularly and never moved — except in one eye.

At last Mr. Tod's preparations were complete. The pail was full of water; the rope was tightly strained over the top of the bed, and across the window-sill to the tree outside.

"It will make a great mess in my bedroom; but I could never sleep

Contraption for the trapping of Tommy Brock,

a most troublesome and presumptuous individual of whom i seek to be Rid.

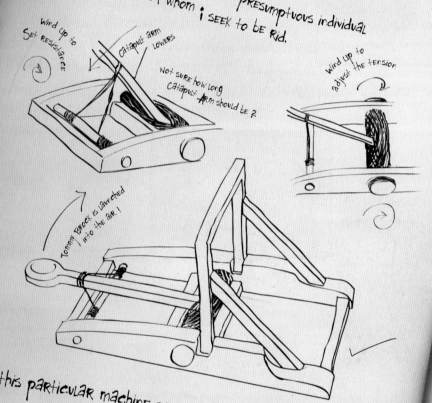

Wind up to set resistance

Catapult arm lowers

Not sure how long catapult arm should be ?

Wind up to adjust the tension

Tommy Brock is launched into the air !

NB: this particular machine proved less than perfect. The speed and distance levers need some adapting. Mr. Brock flew far further than i had anticipated and caused quite considerable damage in front of my winter earth dwelling. Upon landing, this most DISAGREEABLE of fellows appeared to drop through the ground and land in an odd sort of tunnel that seemed to stop directly beneath my kitchen, and lead nowhere. The tunnel smelled strongly of rabbit although none could be found.

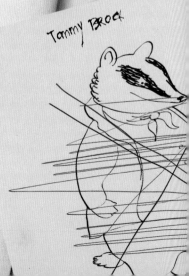

Tommy Brock

THE TALE OF
TIMMY TIPTOES

ONCE UPON A TIME there
was a little fat comfortable
grey squirrel, called Timmy
Tiptoes. He had a nest thatched
with leaves in the top of a tall
tree; and he had a little squirrel
wife called Goody.

Timmy Tiptoes sat out,
enjoying the breeze; he whisked
his tail and chuckled — "Little
wife Goody, the nuts are ripe;
we must lay up a store for
winter and spring."

Goody Tiptoes was busy
pushing moss under the
thatch — "The nest is
so snug, we shall be sound
asleep all winter." "Then
we shall wake up all the
thinner, when there is
nothing to eat in
spring-time," replied
prudent Timothy.

When Timmy and Goody
Tiptoes came to the nut
thicket, they found other
squirrels were there already.

Timmy took off his jacket
and hung it on a twig;
they worked away quietly
by themselves.

Every day they made
several journeys and
picked quantities of nuts.
They carried them away
in bags, and stored them
in several hollow stumps
near the tree where they
had built their nest.

When these stumps were full, they began to empty the bags into a hole high up a tree, that had belonged to a wood-pecker; the nuts rattled down — down — down inside.

"How shall you ever get them out again? It is like a money-box!" said Goody.

"I shall be much thinner before spring-time, my love," said Timmy Tiptoes, peeping into the hole.

They did collect quantities — because they did not lose them!

Squirrels who bury their nuts in the ground lose more than half, because they cannot remember the place.

The most forgetful squirrel in the wood was called Silvertail. He began to dig, and he could not remember. And then he dug again and found some nuts that did not belong to him; and there was a fight. And other squirrels began to dig — the whole wood was in commotion!

Unfortunately, just at this time a flock of little birds flew by, from bush to bush, searching for green caterpillars and spiders. There were several sorts of little birds, twittering different songs.

The first one sang — "Who's bin digging-up *my* nuts? Who's-been-digging-up *my* nuts?"

And another sang — "Little bit-a-bread and-*no*-cheese! Little bit-a-bread an'-*no*-cheese!"

The squirrels followed and listened. The first little bird flew into the bush where Timmy and Goody Tiptoes were quietly tying up their bags, and it sang — "Who's-bin digging-up *my* nuts? Who's been digging-up *my*-nuts?"

Timmy Tiptoes went on with his work without replying; indeed, the little bird did not expect an answer. It was only singing its natural song, and it meant nothing at all.

But when the other squirrels heard that song, they rushed upon Timmy Tiptoes and cuffed and scratched him, and upset his bag of nuts. The innocent little bird which had caused all the mischief, flew away in a fright!

Timmy rolled over and over, and then turned tail and fled towards his nest, followed by a crowd of squirrels shouting — "Who's-been digging-up *my*-nuts?"

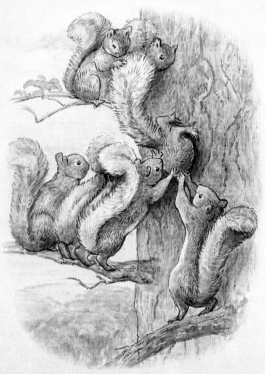

They caught him and dragged him up the very same tree, where there was the little round hole, and they pushed him in. The hole was much too small for Timmy Tiptoes' figure. They squeezed him dreadfully, it was a wonder they did not break his ribs. "We will leave him here till he confesses," said Silvertail Squirrel, and he shouted into the hole —

"Who's-been-digging-up *my*-nuts?"

Timmy Tiptoes made no
reply; he had tumbled down
inside the tree, upon half a
peck of nuts belonging to
himself. He lay quite stunned
and still.

Goody Tiptoes picked up
the nut bags and went home.
She made a cup of tea for
Timmy; but he didn't come
and didn't come.

Goody Tiptoes passed a
lonely and unhappy night.
Next morning she ventured
back to the nut-bushes
to look for him; but the
other unkind squirrels
drove her away.

She wandered all over the
wood, calling —

"Timmy Tiptoes! Timmy
Tiptoes! Oh, where is
Timmy Tiptoes?"

She led the way to the wood-pecker's tree, and they listened at the hole.

Down below there was a noise of nut crackers, and a fat squirrel voice and a thin Chipmunk[*] voice were singing together —

> "My little old man and I fell out,
> How shall we bring this matter
>   about?
> Bring it about as well as you can,
> And get you gone, you little
>   old man!"

"You could squeeze in, through that little round hole," said Goody Tiptoes. "Yes, I could," said the Chipmunk, "but my husband, Chippy Hackee, bites!"

Down below there was a noise of cracking nuts and nibbling; and then the fat squirrel voice and the thin Chipmunk[*] voice sang —

> "For the diddlum day
>   Day diddle dum di!
>   Day diddle diddle dum day!"

In the original version of the tale, Beatrix used the word 'squirrel' here. We have respectfully changed it to 'chipmunk'.

Then Goody peeped in at
the hole, and called down
— "Timmy Tiptoes! Oh fie,
Timmy Tiptoes!" And Timmy
replied, "Is that you, Goody
Tiptoes? Why, certainly!"

He came up and kissed
Goody through the hole; but he
was so fat that he could
not get out.

Chippy Hackee was not
too fat, but he did not want
to come; he stayed down
below and chuckled.

And so it went on for a
fortnight; till a big wind
blew off the top of the
tree, and opened up the
hole and let in the rain.

Then Timmy Tiptoes
came out, and went home
with an umbrella.

But Chippy Hackee continued to camp out for another week, although it was uncomfortable.

At last a large bear came walking through the wood. Perhaps he also was looking for nuts; he seemed to be sniffing around.

Chippy Hackee went home in a hurry!

And when Chippy Hackee got home, he found he had caught a cold in his head; and he was more uncomfortable still.

And now Timmy and Goody Tiptoes keep their nut-store
fastened up with a little padlock.

And whenever that little bird sees the Chipmunks, he sings —
"Who's-been-digging-up *my*-nuts? Who's been digging-up
my-nuts?" But nobody ever answers!

THE END

Prior to his safe return, Goody Tiptoes had tried everything to find her lost husband . . . ⟶

MISSING

My husband, TIMMY TIPTOES.

Bright shiny eyes

Red jacket
(Buttons missing from jacket)

A little portly (stomach)

Last seen beneath this **Very** tree, tying up **nut bags** in preparation for Storage before being chased by **Silvertail** Squirrel and others.

- He is a little plump, and Very friendly
- Does Not normally bite

Contact: **Goody Tiptoes**, The Thatched Nest, Sweeping Oak

THE TALE OF
PIGLING
BLAND

ONCE UPON A TIME there was an old pig called Aunt Pettitoes. She had eight of a family: four little girl pigs, called Cross-patch, Suck-suck, Yock-yock and Spot; and four little boy pigs, called Alexander, Pigling Bland, Chin-chin and Stumpy. Stumpy had had an accident to his tail.

The eight little pigs had very fine appetites — "Yus, yus, yus! they eat and indeed they *do* eat!" said Aunt Pettitoes, looking at her family with pride.

Suddenly there were fearful squeals; Alexander had squeezed inside the hoops of the pig trough and stuck.

Aunt Pettitoes and I dragged him out by the hind legs.

Chin-chin was already in disgrace; it was washing day, and he had eaten a piece of soap. And presently in a basket of clean clothes, we found another dirty little pig — "Tchut, tut, tut! whichever is this?" grunted Aunt Pettitoes.

Now all the pig family are pink, or pink with black spots, but this pig child was smutty black all over; when it had been popped into a tub, it proved to be Yock-yock.

I went into the garden; there I found Cross-patch and Suck-suck rooting up carrots. I whipped them myself and led them out by the ears. Cross-patch tried to bite me.

"Aunt Pettitoes, Aunt Pettitoes! you are a worthy person, but your family is not well brought up. Every one of them has been in mischief except Spot and Pigling Bland."

"Yus, yus!" sighed Aunt Pettitoes. "And they drink bucketfuls of milk; I shall have to get another cow! Good little Spot shall stay at home to do the housework; but the others must go. Four little boy pigs and four little girl pigs are too many altogether. Yus, yus, yus," said Aunt Pettitoes, "there will be more to eat without them."

So Chin-chin and Suck-suck went away in a wheelbarrow, and Stumpy, Yock-yock and Cross-patch rode away in a cart.

roosts, bacon and eggs; always
walk upon your hind legs."
Pigling Bland, who was a
sedate little pig, looked
solemnly at his mother, a
tear trickled down his cheek.

Aunt Pettitoes turned to the
other — "Now son Alexander take
the hand" — "Wee, wee, wee!"
giggled Alexander — "take the hand of your brother Pigling Bland,
you must go to market. Mind —" "Wee, wee, wee!" interrupted
Alexander again. "You put
me out," said Aunt Pettitoes
— "Observe sign-posts and
milestones; do not gobble
herring bones —" "And
remember," said I impressively,
"if you once cross the county
boundary you cannot come
back. Alexander, you are
not attending. Here are two

licences permitting two pigs
to go to market in Lancashire.
Attend, Alexander. I have
had no end of trouble in
getting these papers from the
policeman." Pigling Bland
listened gravely; Alexander
was hopelessly volatile.

I pinned the papers, for safety,
inside their waistcoat pockets;

Aunt Pettitoes gave to each a little bundle, and eight conversation peppermints with appropriate moral sentiments in screws of paper. Then they started.

Pigling Bland and Alexander trotted along steadily for a mile; at least Pigling Bland did. Alexander made the road half as long again by skipping from side to side. He danced about and pinched his brother, singing —

> "This pig went to market, this pig stayed at home,
> This pig had a bit of meat —

"Let's see what they have given *us* for dinner, Pigling?"

He glanced wistfully along the road towards the hills, and then set off walking obediently the other way, buttoning up his coat against the rain. He had never wanted to go; and the idea of standing all by himself in a crowded market, to be stared at, pushed,  and hired by some big strange farmer was very disagreeable —

"I wish I could have a little garden and grow potatoes," said Pigling Bland.

He put his cold hand in his pocket and felt his paper, he put his other hand in his other pocket and felt another paper — Alexander's! Pigling squealed; then ran back frantically, hoping to overtake Alexander and the policeman.

He took a wrong turn — several wrong turns, and was quite lost. It grew dark, the wind whistled, the trees creaked and groaned.

Pigling Bland became frightened and cried "Wee, wee, wee! I can't find my way home!"

After an hour's wandering he got out of the wood; the moon shone through the clouds, and Pigling Bland saw a country that was new to him.

The road crossed a moor; below was a wide valley with a river twinkling in the moonlight, and beyond — in misty distance — lay the hills.

He saw a small wooden hut, made his way to it, and crept inside — "I am afraid it *is* a hen house, but what can I do?" said Pigling Bland, wet and cold and quite tired out.

"Bacon and eggs, bacon and eggs!" clucked a hen on a perch.

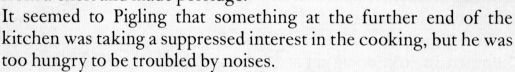

Mr. Piperson pulled off the other boot and flung it after the first, there was again a curious noise — "Be quiet, will ye?" said Mr. Piperson. Pigling Bland sat on the very edge of the coppy stool.

Mr. Piperson fetched meal from a chest and made porridge. It seemed to Pigling that something at the further end of the kitchen was taking a suppressed interest in the cooking, but he was too hungry to be troubled by noises.

Mr. Piperson poured out three platefuls: for himself, for Pigling, and a third — after glaring at Pigling — he put away with much scuffling, and locked up. Pigling Bland ate his supper discreetly.

After supper Mr. Piperson consulted an almanac, and felt Pigling's ribs; it was too late in the season for curing bacon, and he grudged his meal. Besides, the hens had seen this pig.

He looked at the small remains of a flitch, and then looked undecidedly at Pigling. "You may sleep on the rug," said Mr. Peter Thomas Piperson.

Pigling Bland slept like a top. In the morning Mr. Piperson made more porridge; the weather was warmer. He looked to see how much meal was left in the chest, and seemed dissatisfied — "You'll likely be moving on again?" said he to Pigling Bland.

Before Pigling could reply, a neighbour, who was giving Mr. Piperson and the hens a lift, whistled from the gate. Mr. Piperson hurried out with the hamper, enjoining Pigling to shut the door behind him and not meddle with nought; or "I'll come back and skin ye!" said Mr. Piperson.

It crossed Pigling's mind that if *he* had asked for a lift, too, he might still have been in time for market.

But he distrusted Peter Thomas.

After finishing breakfast at his leisure, Pigling had a look round the cottage; everything was locked up. He found some potato peelings in a bucket in the back kitchen. Pigling ate the peel, and washed up the porridge plates in the bucket. He sang while he worked —

> "Tom with his pipe made such a noise,
>   He called up all the girls and boys —
> And they all ran to hear him play,
>   'Over the hills and far away!' "

Suddenly a little smothered voice chimed in —

> "Over the hills and a great way off,
>   The wind shall blow my top knot off!"

Pigling Bland put down a plate which he was wiping, and listened.

After a long pause, Pigling went on tip-toe and peeped round the door into the front kitchen. There was nobody there.

After another pause, Pigling approached the door of the locked cupboard, and snuffed at the keyhole. It was quite quiet.

After another long pause, Pigling pushed a peppermint under the door. It was sucked in immediately.

In the course of the day Pigling pushed in all his remaining six peppermints.

When Mr. Piperson returned, he found Pigling sitting before the fire; he had brushed up the hearth and put on the pot to boil; the meal was not get-at-able.

Mr. Piperson was very affable; he slapped Pigling on the back, made lots of porridge and forgot to lock the meal chest. He did lock the cupboard door; but without properly shutting it. He went to bed early, and told Pigling upon no account to disturb him next day before twelve o'clock.

Pigling Bland sat by the fire, eating his supper.

All at once at his elbow, a little voice spoke — "My name is Pig-wig. Make me more porridge, please!" Pigling Bland jumped, and looked round.

A perfectly lovely little black Berkshire pig stood smiling beside him. She had twinkly little screwed up eyes, a double chin, and a short turned up nose.

She pointed at Pigling's plate; he hastily gave it to her, and fled to the meal chest — "How did you come here?" asked Pigling Bland.

"Stolen," replied Pig-wig, with her mouth full. Pigling helped himself to meal without scruple. "What for?" "Bacon, hams," replied Pig-wig cheerfully. "Why on earth don't you run away?" exclaimed the horrified Pigling.

"I shall after supper," said Pig-wig decidedly.

Pigling Bland made more porridge and watched her shyly.

She finished a second plate, got up, and looked about her, as though she were going to start.

"You can't go in the dark," said Pigling Bland.

Pig-wig looked anxious.

"Do you know your way by daylight?"

"I know we can see this little white house from the hills across the river. Which way are *you* going, Mr. Pig?"

"To market — I have two pig papers. I might take you to the bridge; if you have no objection," said Pigling, much confused and sitting on the edge of his coppy stool. Pig-wig's gratitude was such and she asked so many questions that it became embarrassing to Pigling Bland.

"Come, Pig-wig, we must get to the bridge before folks are stirring." "Why do you want to go to market, Pigling?" inquired Pig-wig presently. "I don't want; I want to grow potatoes." "Have a peppermint?" said Pig-wig. Pigling Bland refused quite crossly. "Does your poor toothy hurt?" inquired Pig-wig. Pigling Bland grunted.

Pig-wig ate the peppermint herself, and followed the opposite side of the road. "Pig-wig! keep under the wall, there's a man ploughing." Pig-wig crossed over, they hurried down hill towards the county boundary.

Suddenly Pigling stopped; he heard wheels.

Slowly jogging up the road below them came a tradesman's cart. The reins flapped on the horse's back, the grocer was reading a newspaper.

"Take that peppermint out of your mouth, Pig-wig, we may have to run. Don't say one word. Leave it to me. And in sight of the bridge!" said poor Pigling, nearly crying. He began to walk frightfully lame, holding Pig-wig's arm.

The grocer, intent upon his newspaper, might have passed them, if his horse had not shied and snorted. He pulled the cart crossways, and held down his whip. "Hallo! Where are *you* going to?" — Pigling Bland stared at him vacantly.

"Are you deaf? Are you going to market?" Pigling nodded slowly.

"I thought as much. It was yesterday. Show me your licence?"

Pigling stared at the off hind shoe of the grocer's horse which had picked up a stone.

The grocer flicked his whip — "Papers? Pig licence?" Pigling fumbled in all his pockets, and handed up the papers. The grocer read them, but still seemed dissatisfied. "This here pig, is a young lady; is her name Alexander?" Pig-wig opened her mouth and shut it again; Pigling coughed asthmatically.

The grocer ran his finger down the advertisement column of his newspaper — "Lost, stolen or strayed, 10s. reward"; he looked suspiciously at Pig-wig. Then he stood up in the trap, and whistled for the ploughman.

"You wait here while I drive on and speak to him," said the grocer, gathering up the reins. He knew that pigs are slippery; but surely, such a *very* lame pig could never run!

"Not yet, Pig-wig, he will look back." The grocer did so; he saw the two pigs stock-still in the middle of the road. Then he looked

over at his horse's heels; it was lame also; the stone took some time to knock out, after he got to the ploughman.

"Now, Pig-wig, NOW!" said Pigling Bland.

Never did any pigs run as these pigs ran! They raced and squealed and pelted down the long white hill towards the bridge. Little fat Pig-wig's petticoats fluttered, and her feet went pitter, patter, pitter, as she bounded and jumped.

They ran, and they ran, and they ran down the hill, and across a short cut on level green turf at the bottom, between pebble beds and rushes.

They came to the river, they came to the bridge — they crossed it hand in hand — then over the hills and far away she danced with Pigling Bland!

THE END

Oh, did you ever see such a happy pair of pigs . . .

Master Pigling Bland and Miss Pig-wig

Request the pleasure of Alexander

At a celebration for their marriage to be held at

Calypso Meadows

on Friday, July 14th at 2pm

R S V P

Troughing and dancing until late

Latecomers will find no food

Formal attire

Dear Alexander,

I do hope this finds you well and happily settled. I trust you have been able to put that unfortunate business with the policeman and the missing pig paper behind you.

You will see that I am to be married, and should be delighted if you could attend the celebrations. My new bride (a lovely black Berkshire pig) and I are much obliged to you, for the pig paper that you lost (I found it in my other pocket) enabled my dearest love to run over the hills and far away with me.

Do you keep up with Aunt Pettitoes, or our brothers and sisters? If so, please do pass on my best regards but be good enough to keep this invitation to yourself. I well remember how much they all eat …

Yours, in anticipation,

Pigling Bland

THE TALE OF
JOHNNY
TOWN-MOUSE

JOHNNY TOWN-MOUSE was born in a cupboard. Timmy Willie was born in a garden. Timmy Willie was a little country mouse who went to town by mistake in a hamper. The gardener sent vegetables to town once a week by carrier; he packed them in a big hamper.

The gardener left the hamper by the garden gate, so that the carrier could pick it up when he passed. Timmy Willie crept in through a hole in the wickerwork, and after eating some peas — Timmy Willie fell fast asleep.

He awoke in a fright, while the hamper was being lifted into the carrier's cart. Then there was a jolting, and a clattering of horse's feet; other packages were thrown in; for miles and miles — jolt — jolt — jolt! and Timmy Willie trembled amongst the jumbled up vegetables.

At last the cart stopped at a house, where the hamper was taken out, carried in, and set down. The cook gave the carrier sixpence; the back door banged, and the cart rumbled away. But there was no quiet; there seemed to be hundreds of carts passing. Dogs barked; boys whistled in the street; the cook laughed, the parlour maid ran up and down-stairs; and a canary sang like a steam engine.

Timmy Willie, who had lived all his life in a garden, was almost frightened to death. Presently the cook opened the hamper and began to unpack the vegetables. Out sprang the terrified Timmy Willie.

Up jumped the cook on a chair, exclaiming "A mouse! a mouse! Call the cat! Fetch me the poker, Sarah!" Timmy Willie did not wait for Sarah with the poker; he rushed along the skirting-board till he came to a little hole, and in he popped.

He dropped half a foot, and crashed into the middle of a mouse dinner party, breaking three glasses. — "Who in the world is this?" inquired Johnny Town-mouse. But after the first exclamation of surprise he instantly recovered his manners.

With the utmost politeness he introduced Timmy Willie to nine other mice, all with long tails and white neckties. Timmy Willie's own tail was insignificant. Johnny Town-mouse and his friends noticed it; but they were too well bred to make personal remarks; only one of them asked Timmy Willie if he had ever been in a trap?

The dinner was of eight courses; not much of anything, but truly elegant. All the dishes were unknown to Timmy Willie, who would have been a little afraid of tasting them; only he was very hungry, and very anxious to behave with company manners.

The continual noise upstairs made him so nervous, that he dropped a plate. "Never mind, they don't belong to us," said Johnny.

"Why don't those youngsters come back with the dessert?" It should be explained that two young mice, who were waiting on the others, went skirmishing upstairs to the kitchen between courses. Several times they had come tumbling in, squeaking and laughing; Timmy Willie learnt with horror that they were being chased by the cat. His appetite failed, he felt faint. "Try some jelly?" said Johnny Town-mouse.

"No? Would you rather go to bed? I will show you a most comfortable sofa pillow."

The sofa pillow had a hole in it. Johnny Town-mouse quite honestly recommended it as the best bed, kept exclusively for visitors. But the sofa smelt of cat. Timmy Willie preferred to spend a miserable night under the fender.

It was just the same next day. An excellent breakfast was provided — for mice accustomed to eat bacon; but Timmy Willie had been reared on roots and salad. Johnny Town-mouse and his friends racketted about under the floors, and came boldly out all over the house in the evening. One particularly loud crash had been caused by Sarah tumbling downstairs with the tea-tray; there were crumbs and sugar and smears of jam to be collected, in spite of the cat.

Timmy Willie longed to be at home in his peaceful nest in a sunny bank. The food disagreed with him; the noise prevented him from sleeping. In a few days he grew so thin that Johnny Town-mouse noticed it, and questioned him. He listened to Timmy Willie's story and inquired about the garden. "It sounds rather a dull place? What do you do when it rains?"

Mister Johnny Town-mouse
Under the skirting (kitchen)
12 Market Street
Hawkshead

Dear Johnny

I do hop this note finds you well, and I also hop the cat has not got you or any of your frends. Thank you for being so kynd when I came too stay. It can't have been easy looking arfter a mouse of such limited ~~orficashun sistikation~~ tastes. I am afraid I could never get used to the noyse and busyness of the town. My nerves are just not up to it. I would love to show you aroond my garden one day, and shall keep a lookout for you when the hamper is droppt on Satterdays.

Kindest regards,
Timmie Willie

My dear Timmy,

Thank you for making me feel so very welcome. It was a relief to find you looking so well and clearly happy in your very small cosy little hole home.

I was most comfortable during my stay, and you are an excellent plain cook. I did find, however, that the general air of damp and continual smell of grass was not really for me, and the silence of the place is quite unnerving.

If you ever again feel the need for a trip to town, I would be delighted to host a dinner party in your honour. Perhaps you could bring some acorns in case of stomach complaints.

With warmest wishes,   Johnny Town-Mouse

PS – there is talk of finding a country home for one of the kittens, so look out.

Mr. Timothy Willie
Sandy Burrow
South-westerley Garden Corner
Mill Cottage
Sawrey

THE TALE OF
SAMUEL WHISKERS

ONCE UPON A TIME there was an old cat, called Mrs. Tabitha Twitchit, who was an anxious parent. She used to lose her kittens continually, and whenever they were lost they were always in mischief!

On baking day she determined to shut them up in a cupboard.

She caught Moppet and Mittens, but she could not find Tom.

Mrs. Tabitha went up and down all over the house, mewing for Tom Kitten. She looked in

the pantry under the staircase, and she searched the best spare bedroom that was all covered up with dust sheets. She went right upstairs and looked into the attics, but she could not find him anywhere.

It was an old, old house, full of cupboards and passages. Some of the walls were four feet thick, and there used to be queer noises inside them, as if there might be a little secret staircase. Certainly there were odd little jagged doorways in the wainscot, and things disappeared at night — especially cheese and bacon.

Mrs. Tabitha became more and more distracted, and mewed dreadfully.

While their mother was searching the house, Moppet and Mittens had got into mischief.

The cupboard door was not locked, so they pushed it open and came out.

"The chimney wants sweeping — Oh, dear me, Cousin Ribby — now Moppet and Mittens are gone!

"They have both got out of the cupboard!"

Ribby and Tabitha set to work to search the house thoroughly again. They poked under the beds with Ribby's umbrella, and they rummaged in cupboards. They even fetched a candle, and looked inside a clothes chest in one of the attics. They could not find anything, but once they heard a door bang and somebody scuttered downstairs.

"Yes, it is infested with rats," said Tabitha tearfully. "I caught seven young ones out of one hole in the back kitchen, and we had them for dinner last Saturday. And once I saw the old father rat — an enormous old rat, Cousin Ribby. I was just going to jump upon him, when he showed his yellow teeth at me and whisked down the hole.

"The rats get upon my nerves, Cousin Ribby," said Tabitha. Ribby and Tabitha searched and searched. They both heard a curious roly-poly noise under the attic floor. But there was nothing to be seen.

They returned to the kitchen. "Here's one of your kittens at least," said Ribby, dragging Moppet out of the flour barrel.

They shook the flour off her and set her down on the kitchen floor. She seemed to be in a terrible fright.

"Oh! Mother, Mother," said Moppet, "there's been an old woman rat in the kitchen, and she's stolen some of the dough!"

The two cats ran to look at the dough pan. Sure enough there were marks of little scratching fingers, and a lump of dough was gone!

"Which way did she go, Moppet?"

But Moppet had been too much frightened to peep out of the barrel again.

Ribby and Tabitha took her with them to keep her safely in sight, while they went on with their search.

They went into the dairy.

The first thing they found was Mittens, hiding in an empty jar.

They tipped up the jar, and she scrambled out.

"Oh, Mother, Mother!" said Mittens —

"Oh! Mother, Mother, there has been an old man rat in the dairy — a dreadful 'normous big rat, Mother; and he's stolen a pat of butter and the rolling-pin."

Ribby and Tabitha looked at one another.

"A rolling-pin and butter! Oh, my poor son Thomas!" exclaimed Tabitha, wringing her paws.

"A rolling-pin?" said Ribby. "Did we not hear a roly-poly noise in the attic when we were looking into that chest?"

Ribby and Tabitha rushed upstairs again. Sure enough the roly-poly noise was still going on quite distinctly under the attic floor.

"This is serious,
Cousin Tabitha," said
Ribby. "We must send
for John Joiner at once,
with a saw."

*

Now this is what had been happening to Tom Kitten, and it shows
how very unwise it is to go up a chimney in a very old house, where
a person does not know his
way, and where there are
enormous rats.

Tom Kitten did not want
to be shut up in a cupboard.
When he saw that his
mother was going to bake,
he determined to hide.

He looked about for a
nice convenient place, and
he fixed upon the chimney.

The fire had only just been lighted, and it was not hot; but
there was a white choky smoke from the green sticks. Tom Kitten
got upon the fender and looked up. It was a big old-fashioned
fire-place.

The chimney itself was wide enough inside for a man to stand up
and walk about. So there was plenty of room for a little Tom Cat.

He jumped right up into the fire-place, balancing himself upon
the iron bar where the kettle hangs.

Tom Kitten took another big jump off the bar, and landed on a ledge high up inside the chimney, knocking down some soot into the fender.

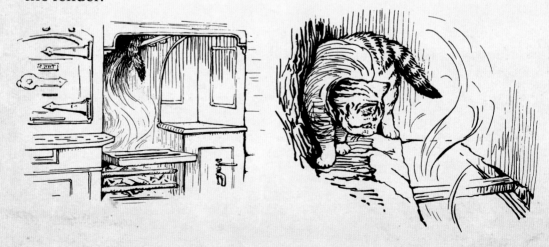

Tom Kitten coughed and choked with the smoke; and he could hear the sticks beginning to crackle and burn in the fire-place down below. He made up his mind to climb right to the top, and get out on the slates, and try to catch sparrows.

"I cannot go back. If I slipped I might fall in the fire and singe my beautiful tail and my little blue jacket."

The chimney was a very big old-fashioned one. It was built in the days when people burnt logs of wood upon the hearth.

The chimney stack stood up above the roof like a little stone tower, and the daylight shone down from the top, under the slanting slates that kept out the rain.

Tom Kitten was getting very frightened! He climbed up, and up, and up.

Then he waded sideways through inches of soot. He was like a little sweep himself.

It was most confusing in the dark. One flue seemed to lead into another.

There was less smoke, but Tom Kitten felt quite lost.

He scrambled up and up; but before he reached the chimney top he came to a place where somebody had loosened a stone in the wall. There were some mutton bones lying about —

"This seems funny," said Tom Kitten. "Who has been gnawing bones up here in the chimney? I wish I had never come! And what a funny smell? It is something like mouse; only dreadfully strong. It makes me sneeze," said Tom Kitten.

He squeezed through the hole in the wall, and dragged himself along a most uncomfortably tight passage where there was scarcely any light.

He groped his way carefully for several yards; he was at the back of the skirting-board in the attic, where there is a little mark * in the picture.

All at once he fell head over heels in the dark, down a hole, and landed on a heap of very dirty rags.

When Tom Kitten picked himself up and looked about him — he found himself in a place that he had never seen before, although he had lived all his life in the house.

It was a very small stuffy fusty room, with boards, and rafters, and cobwebs, and lath and plaster. Opposite to him — as far away as he could sit — was an enormous rat.

"What do you mean by tumbling into my

bed all covered with smuts?" said the rat, chattering his teeth.

"Please, sir, the chimney wants sweeping," said poor Tom Kitten.

"Anna Maria! Anna Maria!" squeaked the rat. There was a pattering noise and an old woman rat poked her head round a rafter. All in a minute she rushed upon Tom Kitten, and before he knew what was happening —

His coat was pulled off, and he was rolled up in a bundle, and tied with string in very hard knots.

Anna Maria did the tying. The old rat watched her and took snuff. When she had finished, they both sat staring at him with their mouths open.

"Anna Maria," said the old man rat (whose name was Samuel Whiskers) — "Anna Maria, make me a kitten dumpling roly-poly pudding for my dinner."

"It requires dough and a pat of butter, and a rolling-pin," said Anna Maria, considering Tom Kitten with her head on one side.

"No," said Samuel Whiskers, "make it properly, Anna Maria, with breadcrumbs."

"Nonsense! Butter and dough," replied Anna Maria.

The two rats consulted together for a few minutes and then went away.

Samuel Whiskers got through a hole in the wainscot, and went boldly down the front staircase to the dairy to get the butter. He did not meet anybody.

He made a second journey for the rolling-pin. He pushed it in front of him with his paws, like a brewer's man trundling a barrel.

He could hear Ribby and Tabitha talking, but they were busy lighting the candle to look into the chest. They did not see him.

Do **YOU** have a

PROBLEM with
RATS?

Mittens and **Moppet Rat Catchers, Ltd.** *can help*

W e are sisters who run an effective, fast and, above all, discreet service.

Our aim is to
RID you of RATS

EVERY TAIL TELLS A STORY!

References supplied.

Find us at:

The Barn
Hill Top Farmhouse
Sawrey

1/SH
Per dozen (negotiable)

Our success is proven: Tails of victims available for perusal. No apptmnt necessary.

THE TAILOR OF GLOUCESTER

Check thoroughly for cat hairs

Wedding coat for Mayor of Gloucester – required 25th. Midday latest.

No dirty paws!

No napping!

Need pink twist.

Hem to here

Line in lavender silk

Blue running low.

More leaves here (to embroider)

Try to turn into yellow flower. Apologies.

Became distracted.

Five buttons to sew

Buttonhole here

THE TALE OF
GINGER AND
PICKLES

But there is no money in what is called the "till".

The customers came in crowds every day and bought quantities, especially the toffee customers. But there was always no money; they never paid for as much as a pennyworth of peppermints.

But the sales were enormous, ten times as large as Tabitha Twitchit's.

As there was always no money, Ginger and Pickles were obliged to eat their own goods.

Pickles ate biscuits and Ginger ate a dried haddock.

They ate them by candle-light after the shop was closed.

When it came to Jan. 1st there was still no money, and Pickles was unable to buy a dog licence.

"It is very unpleasant, I am afraid of the police," said Pickles.

"It is your own fault for being a terrier; *I* do not require a licence, and neither does Kep, the collie dog."

"It is very uncomfortable, I am afraid I shall be summoned. I have tried in vain to get a licence upon credit at the Post Office," said Pickles. "The place is full of policemen. I met one as I was coming home.

"Let us send in the bill again to Samuel Whiskers, Ginger, he owes 22/9 for bacon."

"I do not believe that he intends to pay at all," replied Ginger.

"And I feel sure that Anna Maria pockets things — Where are all the cream crackers?"

"You have eaten them yourself," replied Ginger.

Ginger and Pickles retired into the back parlour.

They did accounts. They added up sums and sums, and sums.

"Samuel Whiskers has run up a bill as long as his tail; he has had an ounce and three-quarters of snuff since October.

"What is seven pounds of butter at 1/3, and a stick of sealing wax and four matches?"

"Send in all the bills again to everybody 'with comp^{ts}'," replied Ginger.

— sucking his sore fingers and
peering down into the water —
a *much* worse thing happened;
a really *frightful* thing it would
have been, if Mr. Jeremy had
not been wearing a macintosh!

A great big enormous trout
came up — ker-pflop-p-p-p!
with a splash —

— and it seized Mr. Jeremy with
a snap, "Ow! Ow! Ow!" — and
then it turned and dived down
to the bottom of the pond!

But the trout was so displeased
with the taste of the macintosh,
that in less than half a minute it spat
him out again; and the only thing it
swallowed was Mr. Jeremy's goloshes.

Mr. Jeremy bounced up to the surface of the water, like a cork and the bubbles out of a soda water bottle; and he swam with all his might to the edge of the pond.

He scrambled out on the first bank he came to, and he hopped home across the meadow with his macintosh all in tatters.

"What a mercy that was not a pike!" said Mr. Jeremy Fisher.

"I have lost my rod and basket; but it does not much matter, for I am sure I should never have dared to go fishing again!"

He put some sticking plaster on his fingers, and his friends both came to dinner. He could not offer them fish, but he had something else in his larder.

Sir Isaac Newton wore his black and gold waistcoat.

And Mr. Alderman Ptolemy Tortoise brought a salad with him in a string bag.

And instead of a nice dish of minnows — they had a roasted grasshopper with ladybird sauce; which frogs consider a beautiful treat; but *I* think it must have been nasty!

THE END

After such frightening experiences, Jeremy never left home without his nifty map . . .

A Map of Hot Spots and Not Spots

N

Sir Isaac Newton's house

My house

Here is where I was almost supper for a trout.

Good spot for lunch

Good spot for catching minnows

Best place to keep my boat. What a fine boat it is!

Jack Sharp the stickleback lives here

or here if no luck

Family of water rats live here. Keep away!

Good spot for lunch

Mr. Ptolemy's vegetable garden

Mr. Alderman Ptolemy's house

Best place for digging worms
For bait, naturally

THE END